Surprise!

PUFFIN BOOKS
Published by the Penguin Group
Penguin Books USA Inc., 375 Hudson Street, New York, New York 10014, U.S.A.
Penguin Books Ltd, 27 Wrights Lane, London W8 5TZ, England
Penguin Books Australia Ltd, Ringwood, Victoria, Australia
Penguin Books Canada Ltd, 10 Alcorn Avenue, Toronto, Ontario, Canada M4V 3B2
Penguin Books (N.Z.) Ltd, 182–190 Wairau Road, Auckland 10, New Zealand

Penguin Books Ltd, Registered Offices: Harmondsworth, Middlesex, England

First published in the United States of America by Viking Penguin Inc., 1988
Published simultaneously in Canada
Published in a Puffin Easy-to-Read edition, 1996

3 5 7 9 10 8 6 4 2

Text copyright © Jane Fine, 1988
Illustrations copyright © Mary Morgan, 1988
All rights reserved

The Library of Congress has cataloged the Viking edition as follows:
Fine, Jane.
Surprise!/Jane Fine; pictures by Mary Morgan.
p. cm.—(Hello reading!)
Summary: A surprise is in store as three children
prepare breakfast in bed for their mother.
ISBN 0-670-82036-9
[Mothers—Fiction.] I. Morgan, Mary, ill. II. Title.
III. Series: Ziefert, Harriet. Hello reading; 11.
PZ7.Z487Sv   1988b   [E]—dc19   87-26217   CIP   AC

Reprinted by arrangement with Penguin Books USA Inc.

Printed in the United States of America

Reading Level 1.6

Surprise!

Jane Fine
Pictures by Mary Morgan

PUFFIN BOOKS

Everyone is sleeping
in this house.

It is time to wake up.

First Sam gets out of bed—
very quietly.

Next Meg gets out of bed—
very quietly.

And then Jo gets
out of bed.

"Quiet, Jo!"

Sam and Meg and Jo
tiptoe down the stairs.

"Quiet, cat!" says Jo.

They all tiptoe
into the kitchen.

Sam gets a tray.

Meg gets a plate.
Jo gets a mug.

Juice on the tray.
Cookies on the tray.
Flowers on the tray.

Cat on the tray!

Get down, cat!

Sam and Meg and Jo
tiptoe up the stairs—
very quietly.

They put the
tray down—
very quietly.

Sam and Meg and Jo
tiptoe to their rooms.

Sam says, "I have mine."
Meg says, "I have mine!"
Jo says, "I have mine, too!"

Juice on the tray.
Cookies on the tray.
Flowers on the tray.

Three presents
on the tray!

Knock on the door.

"Time to wake up!"
yell Sam and Meg and Jo
very loudly.

Surprise!
Happy Birthday!